The Night Run

First published 2014 by
A & C Black, an imprint of Bloomsbury Publishing Plc
50 Bedford Square, London, WC1B 3DP
www.bloomsbury.com
Bloomsbury is a registered trademark of Bloomsbury Publishing plc

ISBN 978-1-4729-0436-2

A CIP catalogue for this book is available from the British Library.

Printed and bound by CPI Group (UK) Ltd, Croydon CR0 4YY

1 3 5 7 9 10 8 6 4 2

MIX
Paper from
responsible sources
FSC® C020471

The Night Run

Bali Rai

A & C BLACK
AN IMPRINT OF BLOOMSBURY
LONDON NEW DELHI NEW YORK SYDNEY

CONTENTS

Chapter One

The Next Morning

Amritsar, Punjab, Northern India
April 10th 1919

My home city, Amritsar, is smouldering. There was a riot overnight – a curfew has been imposed – and now the streets are beginning to come to life again.

Smoke rises from charred buildings, some still burning. I can taste the ashes in my mouth; feel the kerosene fumes stinging my eyes. In a moment, I will leave this place, perhaps forever.

My mother, heavily pregnant, loads the last of our things onto the cart that our neighbour Mr Khan has given us. He's given us a bullock too, a tall, grey beast with long, curling horns and milky eyes. It will pull us to our new home. Mr Khan looks sad, and his wife is crying. She hugs me tightly and tells me she is sorry. But our troubles aren't her fault. She is not to blame.

In the distance, I watch another woman walk away. She wears a black shawl and there is purpose in her stride. I wish I could run to her but there is no time. Another storm is coming to take the city – another tragedy caused by humans. We have to be away before it strikes.

Chapter Two

Arrest

I think I should explain.

A day earlier, just after five in the evening, British soldiers took my father. He runs a food stall and is a fine and noble man. His name is Mit Singh, and he is my hero. The soldiers didn't care about that. They didn't stop to ask, or to investigate. They simply came, four of them with their rifles, and took my dad away.

We were packing up for the day. My father sells savouries and spiced tea, and each night I hand out leftovers to the poor, who crowd the narrow lanes around the marketplace. My city, Amritsar, is a hectic, noisy, smelly, colourful place. And nowhere is busier than the market. The stalls sell everything from cotton and silk, to birdcages, spices, earthenware pots and fruit. It is the only school I've ever known, and it is my favourite place in the world. Or it was – until they took my dad.

When I returned to the stall, I could see something was wrong. Soldiers surrounded my father.

'I did not riot!' my dad shouted at them. 'You are mistaken!'

The lead soldier, a tall Indian with dark, pockmarked skin and a curling black moustache, told my dad to keep quiet.

'But you have the wrong man!' my father protested.

The soldier raised his rifle and used the butt to hit my father on the head. My dad fell backwards, crying out in pain, and I felt my stomach churn.

'Leave him alone!' I yelled but no one heard me.

The other stallholders had crowded round. Most were friends but none helped my dad. They were too scared. Earlier in the day, rumours had begun of a riot. The rumours were true. People had died and buildings had been burned to the ground. The soldiers were searching for rioters and no one wanted to get in their way. The British ruled India with an iron fist. Anyone who stood against them paid a heavy price.

'Help him!' I shouted. 'Please!'

The lead soldier shook his head.

'We have witnesses,' he said. 'You are a rioter!'

I pushed through the crowd, trying to reach my dad, but two strong, rough hands grabbed me around the shoulders and I was pulled back. It was Atar Khan, one of our neighbours.

'No, Arjan,' he warned. 'Do not make them even angrier, son.'

Hot, salty tears poured down my cheeks. My head felt light. I didn't care what the soldiers did to me. I wanted to help my dad. I struggled in my neighbour's grip.

'You are twelve,' Mr Khan whispered in my ear. 'You are not a man. Stop.'

The crowd grew bigger, and people were shouting. 'Stop the British! Kill the British!' they screamed.

The soldiers began to panic, their eyes frantic and their foreheads sweaty. I felt my heart surge. Perhaps the crowd would free my dad. But then a whistle sounded and three white men arrived, with batons drawn. Behind them came several policemen.

'Disperse immediately!' came the order.

The mob took fright. People began to walk away. I tried to catch sight of my father but it was impossible. Then, as the crowd thinned, I saw the soldiers lift and handcuff him. They led him across the market square and towards the central police station. He turned his face to mine and I saw tears in his eyes. I tried to follow but Mr Khan's grip was too powerful.

'No, son!' he warned again. 'Come, I will take you home. We must inform your mother.'

I shook my head, as more tears came.

'What can she do?' I asked my neighbour. 'We have to help him now!'

Mr Khan paid no attention. Instead, he led me through a maze of narrow and dark back streets; to the small house I shared with my family. His face was set, his expression full of sorrow. He did not speak until we reached my house.

'There's nothing we can do tonight,' he said. 'You need to look after your mother. My cousin cooks for the chief of police. I'll go and speak to him later.'

My mother's face fell as she opened the door.

'Mr Khan?' she asked. 'What's the matter? Where is my husband?'

'There's been a mistake,' Mr Khan told her. 'The British have arrested Arjan's father. They claim he is a rioter.'

My mum, eight months pregnant, cried out and began to faint. Mr Khan grabbed her and held her steady. 'Arjan, bring water – quickly!'

As I ran to find the water urn, Mrs Khan appeared. 'What's all the noise about?'

The Khans lived in the same yard as us, across the narrow court. They were kind and friendly, their own children now adults. As Mr Khan explained the problem to his wife, I held the cup to my mother's lips. Her pale brown eyes were wide with fright.

'We have to help him,' she whispered to me. 'If we don't, the British will kill him.'

The thought made me shudder with fear. I could not imagine a world without my father. I did not want a world without him. Who would teach me how to be a man? Who would look after my mother and my new brother or sister? What would we eat?

Mrs Khan came and sat by my side.

'Go and secure the gates to the yard,' she told me. 'I will look after her.'

I handed the cup over and stood. My legs felt like jelly. Out in the yard, Mr Khan explained what he would do. From the streets, I heard the faint sound of soldiers shouting through loudhailers.

'The *Engrezi* have called a curfew,' Mr Khan told me. 'No one may leave their houses tonight. The penalty for disobeying will be arrest and jail. Perhaps even death.'

'*Engrezi*' is the word for British in our language, Punjabi. They have ruled my country since long before my birth and they will never leave. At least that's what I hear the adults say. I have never understood why they rule us. Surely Indians should rule India? It makes no sense – like a fox taking charge over chickens. It is unnatural. But it is the way things are.

'Tomorrow, at sunrise, I will go to my cousin,' Mr Khan continued. 'He will help us.'

He took me in his arms and gave me a hug.

'Don't worry, son,' he said. 'We will make things right in the morning. For tonight, you need to stay here and take care of your mother.'

I nodded slowly but I couldn't help thinking about my dad. I had never seen him cry before and it felt wrong. His face, as the soldiers took him, would never leave my memory.

'We are just across the way,' my neighbour added. 'Ask if you need anything at all.'

As Mrs Khan continued to watch my mother, I sat on my mattress and cried.

Chapter Three

No-one To Help

Later, the other neighbours began to return. Six families lived around our rectangular paved courtyard, two on each side and two at the rear. A water pump sat in the middle, and a toilet and wash area near the entrance gate. It was crowded and noisy but it was my home. Now, without my dad, it felt like an entirely different place.

My mum and Mrs Khan were talking and brewing tea, so I went outdoors. Darkness had begun to fall, and in the distance I heard gunshots and shouting. I wondered what was happening.

I saw Lala Ram, another neighbour, whispering to Mr Khan. I sneaked past them and into the latrine, before hiding behind the door. Despite the smell, I stayed put, trying to hear their conversation. There was a crack in the door and I watched them through it. They were talking about my father.

'There are rumours, brother,' Lala Ram said to Mr Khan.

Lala had very dark skin and black eyes. He was middle-aged and very skinny, and always rode his bike everywhere. He was a farm hand, working in the fields that surrounded the city. His face was grimy with dust and heat.

'What rumours?' Mr Khan asked him.

Lala Ram shook his head, and leant closer.

'Mit Singh and the others will be taken away from the city,' he explained.

My heart sank and I felt cold. What did he mean?

'I saw the postmaster,' Lala continued. 'The British have arrested twenty men since the rioting began. The banks have been looted and people killed. Revolutionaries are attacking the police. The city is in turmoil, brother.'

Mr Khan looked shocked.

'But Mit Singh is innocent!' he declared. 'We were at the market all day, together!'

Lala Ram shrugged and when he spoke I saw his teeth in the glow of a kerosene lamp, yellow and rotten from the tobacco he chewed regularly.

'The *Engrezi* don't care,' he said. 'They are moving the prisoners on the night train to Lahore. In the morning the prisoners will be taken to court. If found guilty, brother, they will hang for sure!'

My stomach somersaulted and a shiver worked its way across my chest. I felt sick.

'No, no!' said Mr Khan. 'This is an outrage. What will the poor woman do without her husband? Her son is just a child. They will be left destitute!'

Lala Ram shrugged once more.

'They and many others, brother,' he said. 'It is the will of God – what can we do?'

Something dawned on me. A simple, frightening truth. No one would save my father. He would be taken away before sunrise. He would have no escape.

'I want to go out now,' Mr Khan said. 'But how can I risk my own life to save that of Mit Singh?'

Lala Ram nodded.

'There is nothing we can do,' he said. 'Fate will play its own game.'

As the two men walked away, I shook my head. How could this be happening to us? How could I let it happen?

* * *

An hour later, the yard was almost silent. I sat up in bed, and heard my mother breathing gently in her sleep. Over by the simple hearth, I saw a knife, matches and some cold tea. I dressed quickly, drank the tea and took the blade and matches. Tip-toeing across the room, I kissed my mother on her cheek. Her long, chestnut hair fell across her face. She stirred slightly but didn't wake. I stared at her for a long time.

'By morning,' I eventually whispered, 'you will still have a husband and a son. I swear to you, Mother.'

And then, despite the cold and the fear, I climbed a set of wooden ladders, on to Mr Khan's dwelling. The gates to our yard were padlocked shut. The only way out was across the rooftops. Somewhere nearby a fox whined and rats shrieked. An amber glow lit the sky to the east, the remnants of the fires started by the rioters.

I took a deep breath and set off to find my father.

Chapter Four

The Patrol

The darkness made my journey across the rooftops slow. I took each step with care. One mistake and I would fall. My breathing was heavy and I was sweating. Every little noise scared me. The clouds above me were deep purple and midnight blue, and the smell of burning filled my nostrils.

I went east, towards the centre of the city. There were only two places my father could be – the police station or the army barracks. If they were sending him away, I guessed the army would have him. They were closest to the railway station. But I decided to check the police cells anyway. It was on my route, and I could have been wrong.

Eventually, some eight alleys from my own house, I dropped down to the street. It was narrow and paved with cobbles, and stank of human waste. I waited in the shadows, listening for any sign of soldiers or policemen. When I heard nothing, I moved on. I couldn't see a thing and had to feel my way to the main road, using the walls as a guide. The city is home to thousands of rats, and I heard them scurrying about. One slid over my feet as I stepped across an open sewer.

At the main road, I turned right. The street was dark, like the alleyways behind me, but my eyes soon adjusted. I saw nothing and moved on, realising that I had no plan. When I reached the police station, I had had no idea what I would do. Even if they held my father inside, how would I get him out?

My desire to save him had stopped me thinking straight. Now the urgency and determination I'd had at home began to seep away. I had to make a plan, and fast.

The street led to a crossroads, and one of Amritsar's busiest routes. To my left the road went north, towards Lahore some thirty miles away. To the right were the city and the marketplace. The main road looked deserted but I knew that meant nothing. The British sent out regular patrols and I'd heard many stories of the bandits and evil men who prowled the city late into the night. I had to watch my step.

Instead of the fastest route, I went straight on, hoping to avoid trouble. At the heart of the junction I found a barricade. Tables and chairs had been piled high, as though a bonfire was being built. Underneath was straw and other kindling. The fire hadn't been lit. I wondered why, as I heard an owl screech somewhere above me.

I entered more narrow streets, each overcrowded with alleys and yards, and housing. The air was cooling but still warm enough to make me sweat.

As I moved, I thought about the police station. It was a big building, with several entrances. The cells were near the rear wall, and underground. The policemen had a wicked reputation. They were evil and many took bribes. Every week, the market traders had stories to tell about people beaten and tortured by the officers. I shuddered as I recalled the tales. I couldn't bear the thought of my dad being hurt.

Once at the station, I had to check the cells somehow. But how would I get inside? I decided that I would need a distraction – something to send the officers elsewhere, as I sneaked into the back entrance. But I had no idea what that diversion would be.

I went through possibilities in my head as I approached an orphanage. It was weird seeing the city so empty. I'd only ever known Amritsar to be busy, but then I'd never been out so late before. The sounds I was used to during the day were missing, and the atmosphere was eerie. It felt wrong. Then, as I was deciding which way to go, I heard them.

Soldiers.

Panicked and scared, I jumped the wall of the orphanage. The grounds to the back were open and led across some common land into another maze of streets. If I had to, I could run that way. I crouched by the wall first, however, waiting for the patrol to pass by. I could hear their boots as they walked. When I sneaked a look, I saw three of them, with rifles on their shoulders and cigarettes hanging from their mouths. Each wore a red turban and khaki uniform. Each looked bored, too.

'This is a waste of time,' said one, as they walked past my hiding place. 'No one will be out tonight. They aren't stupid.'

'Vigilance,' said a second, in a tone that said he was the leader. 'We must remain on the look-out. The revolutionaries use the darkness to move around.'

'If I see one,' the first replied, 'I'll shoot him on sight. There's no danger.'

The soldiers laughed and one of them started to cough. I felt something near my hand, and my heart began to pound. Fur and feet and...

'*Ow!*' I screamed as a rat bit one of my fingers.

The soldiers stopped. I jumped up and ran, desperate to get away.

'There!' yelled one of the soldiers. 'We have our first criminal!'

I heard them climb over the wall and start the chase. My heart raced as I ran. I was in desperate trouble.

Chapter Five

Running for Cover

I ran for the common behind the orphanage. The ground was uneven and overgrown with weeds. In the darkness, and in my haste, I had no way of knowing where the potholes and divots were. Two open sewers crossed the common – I hoped I wouldn't fall into one. I could hear the soldiers behind me, swearing and shouting, and I prayed they wouldn't try to shoot me.

As I ran, dogs began to bark somewhere nearby. They were almost as scary as the soldiers. Most were wild and roamed in packs at night, attacking the unwary. But I didn't have time to think about them. Not yet. The soldiers were falling behind and I needed to find a hiding place quickly.

Buildings surrounded the common. The only way out was through one of the many exit gates. Most of these would be locked but at the far end, the walls had foot- and handholds, where blocks had been removed. I had often seen people use these to scale up to the rooftops. That was my aim – to lose the soldiers and move on. The barking grew closer and then I heard a gunshot.

The air around me seemed to part as the bullet sped past. I heard it twang off the wall, and dived for cover. I fell amongst tall weeds and crawled away. My heart was pounding even harder. I couldn't let them catch me – not so soon. I had to get to my father.

The soldiers closed in and I could hear their words clearly. They were calling me names, and insulting my mother. I wanted to jump up and confront them but that would have been foolish. I was the only hope my father had. I couldn't let pride ruin that.

The shot had scared the dogs off, but that didn't help me at all. A pack of rabid and hungry mutts would have distracted the soldiers. Now they had only me to concentrate on. I moved away as fast as I could, but there was nowhere to go – only more weeds. The ground smelt damp and earthy and I could feel insects biting at my hands and face.

'He's here somewhere!' the lead soldier shouted. 'Get him!'

I took a deep breath and moved on, wishing that I could fall through a hole somehow and hide. Amazingly, God seemed to answer my prayers. My fingers seemed to push through a mound of earth, finding a hollow. It felt deep and wide and I crawled in. It must have been an abandoned fox den or something similar. I didn't care. I curled up, barely fitting, and waited.

The soldiers were soon around me, whacking through the weeds with their rifles. Any minute they would find me, hiding like an animal, and then my quest would fail. I cursed my pursuers and myself. Why couldn't they just leave? What harm could I do?

'Nothing here, sir,' said one of the soldiers. 'Just weeds and rubble.'

'He has to be here,' said their leader. 'He didn't just vanish!'

They searched a while longer before walking away. I waited until I couldn't hear their voices, perhaps another ten or fifteen minutes, before moving on again. The further away I got, the calmer I became. Soon, I was near the rear buildings and ready to climb up to the rooftops.

I sat up and looked around. Sensing no danger, I jumped to my feet and felt the wall in front of me. I found a gap and then another and began to haul myself upwards. I moved slowly, careful to make sure my grip was secure. Slowly but surely, I worked my way to the roof, and once there, I lay down and shut my eyes, trying to slow my breathing. My heart pounded in my chest.

Down below, the soldiers had returned. I couldn't hear what they were saying but I did hear the whistle sound. They were calling for more patrols. Soon the lanes around the common would be swarming with more soldiers. I would be trapped up above them, unable to get away. Unless I moved before they arrived.

I stood and made my way to a stone stairwell. The steps led down into a courtyard. I took them, hoping that the street entrance wouldn't be padlocked. But it was – just like the one at home. I went back up and tried another courtyard.

After several failed attempts, I was frustrated and angry. I came to the end of the block, and looked down onto a wider street. A patrol stood to my left, some fifty yards away. Another group of soldiers were directly below me, four men, all smoking.

'The area is secure,' said one of them. 'Whoever this rebel is, tonight will be his last night on earth.'

I only had a vague sense of the time. But I knew enough to realise that it was running out. Both for my father and for me.

Chapter Six

Heera

The wait was agonising. I was desperate to get to the police station but couldn't move. The soldiers didn't leave for half an hour. By that point, I was almost frantic.

I imagined them unlocking the cell doors and cuffing my dad. They would take him to the rear entrance and shove him onto a cart. Then they would wheel their way through the night, heading for the train. My father would call out his innocence, and they wouldn't listen. Once on his way to Lahore, he'd be finished. The British hanged revolutionaries without mercy.

I blinked back tears and saw the patrol below me set off. They went right, and turned down a narrow lane. The street was clear now but I knew that the other patrols were nearby. I searched the roof for signs of a way down. At the edge, I found a rope ladder that had been pulled up and folded. I unravelled it and said a prayer. Then I descended to the street.

Across the road, I saw a gap between two shops. I sprinted across and took cover in the shadows. My injured finger throbbed more insistently but I ignored it. I waited and watched – trying to work out a route in my head. The marketplace was five streets ahead, perhaps a half-mile or so. The soldiers were searching the area around me, so I decided to head for the centre of the city. I had lost too much time to consider another long way around.

I took a deep breath and set off, walking as fast as I could. I took the narrow lanes, and made progress quickly. Soon, I was at the edge of the market – as familiar as my own home. It sat in a square, surrounded by tall buildings that seemed to lean over it, like a canopy. Here, I knew every hiding place, so I relaxed. Even if I saw a patrol, I knew that they would not see me.

I stopped next to a water pump and rested a moment. The silence stood out again. I missed the loud voices, the twittering birds and the clamour of daytime. The only thing that remained was the smell of spices – chilli, cumin, black pepper and cardamom. Each scent hung heavily in the air.

I was now five minutes from the police station. And I needed a proper plan. Somehow, I had to get in and out of the station without being seen. And if my father was being held there, I had to help him escape too. For a moment, I felt foolish but then I thought about my mum and the baby growing in her belly. My determination returned and I left my resting place.

Between the market and the station lay an area of dark passages and lanes so narrow that only one person at a time could pass through. These were where the most immoral of Amritsar's people lived, and the police refused to patrol them after dark. Evil men and lowly women lived lives of crime here, and the stories I'd heard made me anxious. Even though my journey was short, it was going to be dangerous.

As if to highlight my fears, I heard a deep growling. Across the square, a pack of four dogs had appeared. The pack leader was big and powerful and my scent had alerted him. I had the knife in my waistband but it wouldn't help. The blade was too short. I needed a heavy stick to keep the dogs off me. I searched the surrounding area and saw nothing I could use.

The dogs began to move towards me slowly, their tails down and backs arched.

During the day, they stayed on the edges of the marketplace, fearing beatings or worse from the stallholders. But at night, the square and the city was theirs.

I remained calm and began to walk away. A dog had never bitten me and ordinarily they didn't scare me either. But my hands were sweaty and my legs started to shake a little. I wasn't a small child but I wasn't an adult either. And the wild dogs had been known to attack people in the past.

'This way!' I heard a female voice whisper.

My breath caught in my throat and my heartbeat galloped. From the shadows, a woman smiled out at me. She wore a simple black shawl of the finest silk and her face seemed kindly.

'Quickly!' she added. 'They will tear you apart!'

I had no choice but to follow her down one of the lanes. I moved quickly as the dogs began to bark wildly behind us. The woman stopped at a wooden door and opened it.

'Inside, son.'

I did as she said. Just as she closed the door, one of the dogs snapped its jaws and butted against it. I sighed in relief and looked around. We were in a passageway, with stairs opposite us, and rooms to either side.

'What are you doing walking the streets so late?' the woman asked me. There was no anger in her tone, just concern.

'Nothing,' I lied, wary of telling a stranger my business.

The woman led me into a room and lit a candle. Her face was truly beautiful: creamy skin like my mother's and brown eyes so pale that they looked almost golden. When she smiled, I felt like I had been wrapped in soft, white clouds. A mellow perfume followed her everywhere – fresh, thick cream and ripe, juicy mangoes.

'Now, now,' she said. 'Mit Singh did not teach his son to lie.'

I must have gasped because the woman explained, 'I know who you are, Arjan.'

'But I've never seen you before,' I replied.

She smiled again. 'You are a young man. Why would you notice me? But I've seen you around the market, handing out food to the hungry and playing with your friends. It's a wonderful place, isn't it?'

I nodded and felt guilty about misleading her.

'I'm looking for my father,' I said. 'He was taken by the soldiers.'

'I heard about it,' she told me. 'But you are just a boy. Brave, perhaps, but foolish too. How can *you* help him?'

I shrugged then shook my head. 'I don't know. But I must try. Without him, my mother and I are lost.'

The woman considered my words a while.

'So you wish to risk your own life to save your father's?'

I shrugged again. 'I cannot let my father die.'

'The people here call me Heera,' she said. 'Perhaps I can help you.'

'How?' I asked, getting excited.

'Patience,' she replied. 'Now let's see to that injury, shall we?'

I looked down at my wounded and swollen finger. How had she known about it? I hadn't even mentioned the rat bite.

'I notice things about people,' she said, as though she could read my thoughts.

When my confusion showed, she laughed gently.

'Not everything out at night is evil,' she said. 'Now, where did I put that ointment?'

Chapter Seven

Breaking Into Jail

The ointment stopped the pain almost immediately, and I asked her what it was made of.

'Herbs and corn oil,' she said. 'It's a secret blend.'

'Thank you,' I said. 'I don't want to be rude but I have to keep going. My neighbour thinks the *Engrezi* will take my father to Lahore. I have to find him before that happens.'

'And I will try to help,' she said again.

'I don't understand who you are,' I told her. 'Are you a rebel – is *that* why you were out so late?'

She shook her head. 'No, I was helping a friend. Someone in trouble, just like you.'

'Like me?'

She nodded. 'Not the same problem. But a problem nonetheless.'

She asked if I had a plan to save my father and I shook my head.

'I didn't think that far ahead,' I admitted. 'I just knew I had to do something.'

Heera thought a moment before replying.

'The night train to Lahore passes through Amritsar in just over an hour,' she told me. 'It comes from Delhi and is heavily guarded because of the revolutionaries. If we are going to save Mit Singh we must do it now. Once he's on that train, your father is lost.'

'Then we have to get moving,' I said eagerly.

Heera stood at the door and closed her eyes. She reminded me of the holy men I'd seen meditating at festivals.

'They are gone,' she said once her eyes were open.

'Who?'

'The dogs,' she replied. 'Come!'

As we went back into the night, I wondered who she was, this strange woman. I hadn't planned on having a companion. I hadn't planned at all. But being with her made my confidence rise.

* * *

The police station was a tall building that took up the whole block. Its walls were white but had weathered over time and there were sandbags piled around the doors, each guarded by sentries. We stood in the shadows next to a bakery, watching them.

'Two at each entrance,' my new companion told me. 'We'll have to avoid them and go to the rear.'

I nodded.

'The cells are back there,' I replied. 'I've seen the criminals being taken in.'

I followed Heera from shop to shop, careful to match her exact footsteps. When it was time to cross the wide thoroughfare, Heera found a rock and gave it to me.

'You see the tin sign above the surgery in the distance?' she asked.

I peered into the night but could only just make it out.

'Sort of,' I told her. 'But not clearly.'

'Can you hit it with that rock?' she asked.

'I'm not sure but I can try.'

She gave me another of her warm smiles. 'Only those who try can ever succeed. Have a go.'

I played throwing games with my friends all the time. From rotten onions to rubber balls, I was a good shot. But this was something else. All I could make out was a rectangle, sitting in darkness. I felt the weight of the rock in my hand and considered the distance. Then I stepped back, took aim and threw. The rock arced through the air, and for a moment I thought it was too high. Only, at the last minute, it seemed to lose height and clanged against the metal sign. In the quiet, the noise was almost shocking.

'What was that?' a guard shouted, raising his rifle.

Heera ignored them and handed me another rock.

'Now this one,' she whispered. 'Same place.'

The second rock flew out of my hand and this time the noise was louder still. Every guard rushed across, leaving us to make our way down the side of the station unseen.

'We must hurry,' I said to Heera. 'If he isn't here, we'll have to run to the barracks.'

At the rear, a single sentry guarded the door. He looked sleepy and Heera told me to hold my ground.

'I'm going to remove him,' she said.

'How?'

'Leave that to me,' she replied. 'But whatever you do, don't move until I call you. Understood?'

I nodded. Heera turned and walked towards the guard. He didn't see her until she was right next to him. He was startled and began to raise his gun. Heera leant in and whispered something to him. His hands fell to his side and he looked down at his feet. Then, just as she'd promised, he walked away, heading for an alleyway opposite. Heera turned and gestured for me to join her. I moved quickly, wondering if she was some kind of witch. How had she made the policeman walk away? What had she said to him?

'Nothing for your young ears,' she replied when I asked.

'But if the chief finds out, he'll be in trouble,' I said.

Heera grinned.

'Not half as much trouble as he'll be in at home,' she said with a wink.

'Huh?'

'Our friend has been visiting the wife of another officer.'

'Eurrgh!' I said. 'Sorry I asked.'

The two rear gates were each ten feet high and eight feet wide. They were made of thick dark wood and looked heavy. Heera turned the handle on one and it moved about two feet. Just enough space for us to squeeze into the yard behind them. The floor was compacted dirt covered in straw, and the place smelled of farmyard animals and their dung. Twenty feet ahead was the back of the main building. To the left was a pen for horses, and to the right a locked iron door and stairs down to the cells.

'How will we open the door?' I asked her.

'There is a key,' she told me. 'They hide it in the wall.'

She led me over and felt the wall. Very quickly, a single block moved and she pulled it free. Behind were two iron keys on a large ring.

'How could you know that?' I said, amazed but excited too. If my dad was being held here, we would be able to get him out.

'The guard told me.'

'Oh,' I said. 'That was a silly question, then.'

Heera shook her head. 'There are no silly questions. Now let's see if Mit Singh is here, shall we?'

She opened the iron door and we descended the steps. My excitement grew stronger and I wanted to run. Could my dad really be so close to freedom?

Chapter Eight

Fire!

Most of the prisoners were asleep, and the guard had passed out at his post. An empty bottle of whiskey sat on the floor next to him.

Where is my dad?' I whispered, as we walked between cells.

I was desperate to see my dad's face amongst the others, but he wasn't there. Heera checked the last cell before shaking her head.

'Let's go,' I said, all my excitement gone. I felt as though someone had ripped my stomach out. Tears began to form in my eyes.

'I have someone to see,' she said quietly. 'Patience.'

I wanted to shout and scream that my dad was running out of time. Something in her face calmed me down. She walked back to the first cell we'd passed. The air was thick with nasty smells and I could hear damp trickling down the walls. Mice sat by the walls, watching us for signs of threat. Huge cobwebs hung from every corner, throwing scary shadows in the lamplight. It was like a dungeon from my nightmares.

I watched as Heera whispered to a sleeping prisoner. Six men shared the tiny cell, asleep on filthy straw mattresses. I thought she might wake all of them but only one opened his eyes.

'Ssh!' Heera warned. 'Come quickly!'

The teenager, maybe seventeen at most, stood and rearranged his clothes. He picked up his turban and edged to the door.

'I do not understand,' he whispered. 'Who are you?'

Heera shook her head. 'Not now. I will explain later. We need to leave immediately.'

She used the stolen keys and within seconds the young man was free. He joined us as we ascended the steps. At the top, we waited. I heard loud voices from the back gates, and one of the horses was startled. It whinnied and whined, and stamped its feet.

'They're everywhere,' said Heera, looking to the teenager.

My confusion, already deep, became bottomless. Why were we rescuing a stranger? It made no sense at all, unless Heera had lied to me, and she was a rebel. I didn't care if she was – I just wanted my dad.

'The train!' I whispered. 'We've got to go.'

Heera shook her head. 'If they catch us, we will be finished. You go on ahead, Arjan. We will follow.'

She turned to the teenager. 'Are you fit?' she asked him.

He nodded.

'Very well – we'll create a distraction and Arjan can sneak away.'

'But what if you get caught?' I said. 'The police will –'

'Let me worry about that,' she told me. 'I'll meet you at the barracks in fifteen minutes.'

She walked over to the three horses and unlatched the gate to their pen. The spooked horses grew silent as she ushered them out. Behind them, she found a straw bale.

'Take this and place it over there,' she ordered the rescued boy, pointing to the main building.

'What should I do?' I asked.

'Be ready to run,' she replied. 'Wait by the gates!'

She took another bale and placed it next to the first. Then she took the kerosene lamp that was lighting the yard and set fire to the bales.

'Raise the alarm,' she told the other boy. 'Now!'

He did as he was told, as the flames started to catch. 'Come quickly! Fire!' he yelled.

Heera unlocked the gates and I helped her pull them back. I waited for the policemen to run through the gap and arrest us but they didn't get the chance. Heera slapped each horse on its hindquarters and they pushed their way through the gap. Smoke began to fill the courtyard.

'Go!' she told me. 'Now!'

I hesitated for just a moment, and then did as she said. In the confusion, the policemen ignored me. They were too concerned about the blaze. One sounded his whistle. Another shouted for help. 'Bring water!' he screamed.

I didn't look back to see where Heera and the teenager were. I didn't have the time. Instead, I sped off down yet another dark alley, heading for the barracks and the railway station. My mouth felt dry from the smoke and my eyes stung but I didn't care. All I could think of was my dad.

Chapter Nine

Running Into Trouble

I hadn't even considered what I'd do if my dad wasn't at the police station. I'd convinced myself he'd be there. And now that I knew better, it felt like starting again.

I worked my way north, through the biggest maze of streets in the city. This time, I saw quite a few people too. The deeper I went, the more I saw. They were drunkards and beggars and criminals. I passed small groups of men drinking liquor and playing cards. Down one alley each doorway was open and gaudily dressed women stood calling out from tiny rooms. It felt like another city – a secret place that I wasn't supposed to know about. I wondered where the police were. Did the curfew not matter in these places?

As I turned a corner and stepped across a sewer, I bumped into a man. He was short and wide, with huge arms and a shaved head, shaped like a cannonball and covered in a giant scorpion tattoo. A thin cigarette hung from his mouth and he squinted at me.

'You lost, boy?' he growled.

I shook my head and tried to stop my legs from shaking. A knife scar bisected the man's ruined left eye, running down his cheek like a fat, pink worm. He scared me.

'Has someone cut out your tongue?' he added. 'Speak before I slap your face off!'

'I'm just g-going home,' I stammered.

The man began to laugh.

'Home?' he said. 'You're either an idiot or a liar. Which is it?'

A meaty hand shot out and grabbed hold of my shirt. I tried to pull away but he was too strong. He dragged me closer, so that I could smell the liquor on his breath.

'Which is it, boy?' he asked again.

I gulped down air.

'I'm lost!' I protested. 'I don't know where I am.'

The man seemed to accept my reply.

'They call me The Bull,' he said. 'And these alleys belong to me. Whatever you see here is mine – man, woman, animal or child…'

The name sent shivers coursing down my spine. Everyone had heard of this man. He was the most notorious bandit in the whole region. I wanted to run away but I couldn't move.

With his free hand, he pulled a blade from his tunic and held it to my right cheek. 'You look scared, boy. Is something wrong?'

He sneered at me. I tried to pull away from him. I wanted him to let me go. Time was ticking.

'Please!' I begged. 'My mother will be looking for me.'

The sneer turned into an unkind smile. 'She is welcome here,' he said.

I looked away so that he wouldn't see the anger in my eyes. He was disrespecting my mother and I wanted to hit him. But I wasn't stupid. I didn't want to die.

'Please!' I said again, my voice just a whine.

He let me go and put away the knife.

'Run along,' he told me. 'Quickly – before I forget to be kind!'

I sighed with relief and sprinted away. Behind me I could hear him laughing. Several more men, all bandits, watched me pass by. I didn't look at them, praying they would leave me be.

At the end of the alley, I came to a junction. My run-in with The Bull had confused me. I'd lost my bearings. As I tried to work out where I was, one of the dangerous men approached me. He was tall and skinny and his teeth were rotten. He was drunk too and held a half-full bottle of whiskey.

'Drink!' he ordered, grabbing hold of my shoulder.

I shrugged him off and went left.

'Come back!' he shouted after me. 'Be a man!'

I started to run as someone stepped from the shadows ahead. I didn't see the punch until it was too late.

* * *

When I came to, I was lying on a mattress in a dimly lit room. I tried to get up but a shooting pain lanced through my head. I winced before vomiting onto the wooden floor. My mind was spinning and I felt groggy. My face throbbed. I lay back and tried to gather my thoughts. I remembered running from The Bull and the drunken man and then...

I stood slowly and shook my head. Then I went to the door. It was locked and there was no key. The window was shuttered but I tried it anyway. When it didn't budge, I got angry and punched it. I had no idea how long I'd been out, but I knew then that I had missed my chance to save my father. I cursed the bandits and the policemen and the soldiers. I had failed and my father was on his way to Lahore to die.

Chapter Ten

Kidnapped

Maybe an hour later, the door opened and a young girl walked in with water. She looked about my age but her eyes were hard and she scowled at me. Her expression almost hid how pretty she was.

'This is for you,' she said in an unfriendly manner.

'Who are you?' I asked. 'Where am I?'

The girl shook her head. Her eyes were jet black and shone, and her hair fell in greasy curls to her shoulders. She wore a gaudy red outfit, like the women I'd seen on the streets. Her hands were covered in henna tattoos.

'It doesn't matter,' she told me. 'Once they get you, they don't let you go. Not unless someone pays your ransom.'

I felt suddenly faint. The bandits…

'I've been kidnapped?' I asked.

'Clever, aren't you?'

'But my mother has no money,' I began to shout. 'And my father is…'

'What?' she asked.

'He's probably dead.'

The girl's expression softened a little. 'Probably?' she asked, almost teasingly. 'Aren't you sure?'

I shook my head and tried not to cry. 'The British took him,' I explained. 'They said he was a rioter. He's on his way to Lahore on the train. They'll hang him for sure.'

The girl nodded. 'My parents were killed. The bandits raided my village and took me away to serve them. My dad tried to fight but The Bull stabbed him. Then they…' She turned her head away and didn't finish her sentence.

'Help me,' I said to her. 'Please?'

When she turned back to face me, her expression was hard again.

'Why should I?' she asked. 'Who are you to me?'

'I'm just like you,' I told her. 'These men are evil. Come with me – we can run away.'

The girl was about to reply when I heard a familiar coarse voice swearing from the hallway.

'Have you fallen down a sewer, you little pig?' yelled The Bull.

He stepped through the door and smiled at me. It was another evil grin. 'I thought you'd gone,' he said, but I knew he was playing with me. 'Did you change your mind?'

My hand went to the swollen bruise underneath my right eye. 'Your men stopped me,' I told him, although he already knew that.

He eyed my clothes before stepping closer. Grabbing my hands, he studied them too.

'Not a rich boy, then?' he said, looking annoyed.

'My parents have nothing,' I said. 'You're wasting your time. They won't pay a ransom.'

Although my father worked, some days we barely had enough to eat. The British had enforced strict laws and the price of everything was going up. No matter how many hours he worked, things never changed. We weren't starving exactly, and we had a roof over our heads, but things were hard. And now that he was gone…

'Do you know how many lads in my gang were just like you?' The Bull asked.

I shook my head.

'Nearly half of them,' he told me. 'They were kidnapped and their parents couldn't pay so I kept them. Well, I kept the smart ones.' He touched his tunic, right where he kept his knife. 'Those who complained didn't get so lucky. There's many an undiscovered grave out in the fields.'

He grabbed the girl by her hair. I could see she was in pain, but she didn't cry out or make a fuss.

'And this little wench,' he said. 'She is like the other women downstairs. I own *them* too.'

I felt sick but said nothing in reply. I didn't want him to get angry and hurt her. Inside, however, I felt rage burning. He was a monster.

'Now try and rest and I'll be back soon,' he added. 'Then you can tell me where you live and I can pay your mother a visit. See if she wants her little boy back.'

'What if I don't tell you?' I asked.

He touched his ruined left eye.

'Oh,' he said softly, 'you'll talk. My guests always talk.'

He pulled the girl from the room by her hair and shut the door. I heard the key turn in the lock and felt the air leave my chest. How had things gone so wrong?

Chapter Eleven

Shanti

I sat and waited for The Bull to return, but next time the door opened, it was the girl again. Her left eye was bruised and her lip split.

'Did he hit you?' I asked her.

She shrugged. 'He always hits me. It's nothing – not any more. I'm used to it.'

She put a cup of water on the floor. 'What's your name?' she asked, without looking at me.

'Arjan. What's yours?'

She went over to the window and leant against the shutters. 'I'm Shanti.'

'Why do you stay here?' I asked her. 'Why don't you leave?'

She looked down at her grubby clothes. 'Where would I go? At least I have a bed and food here. Out on the streets, I would starve.'

'But you must have family – uncles, aunts…?'

She shook her head. 'I would never go back to them. There is too much…*shame*. The bandits have ruined my life. Now I'm theirs.'

I stood and went to her. 'What about the police?'

'You have a lot to learn,' she said. 'There is a curfew but no policemen or soldiers come here. Why is that, do you think?'

She was right – I didn't know anything about such a life. I didn't want to know.

'He bribes them all,' she explained. 'And they come here for the women and the…' Again, she failed to finish, and this time she was crying.

'Come on,' I whispered to her. 'We can escape and you can come with me. My mother is kind and lovely, and my neighbours too. We will take care of you.'

I didn't know if that was true, but I *had* to get out. And if I did escape, I couldn't leave her behind. She was a child, like me. Living with bandits was no life for her.

'Why would strangers care about me?' she asked, full of suspicion. 'I am nothing to them.'

I shook my head and put a hand on her shoulder. I remembered something Heera had said, and wondered where she was. I doubted that she'd made it out of the police station, but I couldn't be sure. There was something different about her. Something special.

'We're not all the same,' I told Shanti. 'I mean humans. Not everyone you meet at night is evil.'

She gave me a sad look as I heard The Bull shouting. 'Must I take my belt to you again!' he barked from below. 'Get back here and do your chores, wench!'

I looked into her eyes.

'Is this what you want?' I said. 'Truly, with all your heart, for the rest of your life?'

I gave her a hug. She smelled of fried spices and cinnamon sticks and earth. I could feel bones through her clothes.

'Shanti?'

She nodded before wiping her eyes. 'I must go,' she said. 'I'll be back soon, though. My master will go and check on the women soon. When he does, I'll release you.'

'And come with me?' I asked, my spirits rising.

She nodded again.

'But we must escape,' she added. 'If he catches us, we will die.'

I thought about my father and felt my determination rise again. I couldn't save him, but I would not fail Shanti. I would not leave her to slavery.

* * *

After much time passed, I thought perhaps Shanti had changed her mind. But then the key turned in the lock and she entered. She wore trousers and a pale blue shirt, and had wiped the make-up from her face. Her hair was held in a cap. She had nothing else with her.

I checked my waistband but couldn't feel the weapon I'd brought from home. My matches were still in my pocket though.

'They found your knife,' she told me. 'My master took it.'

I shrugged. 'I don't care about that.'

'Will your mother really be kind to me?' she asked, sounding like a little girl.

I nodded, and my heart grew heavy as I thought about my father and the baby that he would never see.

'My mother is full of love,' I told her. 'She is the best mother in the world. She won't turn you away. With my father gone, it will be difficult, but she won't let us down. Maybe we can find your family.'

We worked our way down some dangerously rotten stairs and into a dark corridor. Four doors opened into dimly lit rooms, and I could see men passed out on the floor.

'They keep a potion,' Shanti told me, nodding at the sleeping men. 'They use it to drug women or to kidnap people.'

I raised an eyebrow and Shanti smiled.

'I put the potion in the whiskey,' she explained. 'My master's too.'

Despite my sadness, I grinned at her clever thinking.

'We'll still have to be careful,' she added. 'The streets here are very dangerous.'

'Tonight the whole city is dangerous,' I replied. 'Come on!'

I set out again, wondering what was in store. So far I'd faced and avoided angry soldiers, helped set fire to a police station and been taken by bandits and escaped them. I had failed in my quest, and my heart ached for my father, but I wondered how many other twelve-year-olds had experienced such a night. Surely there were no more surprises left.

Chapter Twelve

Night Train

The journey to the barracks was shorter this time. Barely ten minutes after leaving the bandits' lair, we were watching soldiers at a checkpoint. There were two of them, with bright red turbans and waxed moustaches. They looked bored. Behind them sat an arched entrance and another checkpoint. More soldiers strolled around the perimeter.

Even if I had been on time, there was no way I could have saved my father.

We walked on, careful to remain hidden, and stopping every few moments. The air was chilly now, and Shanti shivered. At a junction between two main roads, we waited to let a patrol pass. They were leading two handcuffed men, the sort of thugs we'd just left behind.

Once the road was clear, we crossed and I found an alleyway that led behind a clothing shop I knew. A man called Gulbaru Singh owned it. He was a nasty piece of work.

I found the rear entrance, and I tried the door. It was locked but rattled in its frame. I pulled three or four times and the tiny lock broke.

'What are you doing?' asked Shanti. 'We aren't thieves.'

I led her inside and found a shawl. Next to it was a box of firecrackers. I pocketed a handful. They might be useful later, if we needed a distraction.

'You're cold,' I told her. 'Besides the man that owns this place is horrible. He beats homeless children and cheats his customers.'

Shanti took the shawl without any more argument and wrapped it around herself. As we left, I was reminded of Heera. I wondered what had happened to her and the teenage boy she'd taken from the police cells.

We crossed another, smaller junction, and walked on to where the road ended at a barrier. Beyond was the track, and to the left, the railway station. The homeless people I'd mentioned in the shop were huddled together along the sides of the tracks. Here and there, one of them stirred and watched us pass. Would this be where my family would end up, I wondered, now that my father was gone?

We passed a few small railway buildings, offices where they kept records and counted the ticket money. After these were bigger warehouses, some of them open and full of more homeless. Finally, we reached the stationmaster's house and, close by, the main entrance to the station. It was always open, even though the trains didn't run all night. We stepped between sleeping families, and on into the ticket hall.

A poster had been tacked to the wall. A meeting would take place on a piece of common land called Jallianwalla Bagh. It was set for April 13th – the Sikh festival of Vaisakhi – just a few days away. The city would be filled with people from surrounding villages, coming to celebrate the holy day at the Golden Temple. Underneath was another poster. This one said that all gatherings were banned until further notice. It was from the British.

Shanti asked me what we were doing and I shook my head.

'I don't know,' I told her. 'I was on my way here to find my father when the bandits got me.'

She looked around the shadowy hall.

'Is this where they brought him?' she asked.

'Yes, the train to Lahore came through here some time ago. I failed him.'

I sat down and felt tears begin to pour down my cheeks. I'd been so caught up with escaping that I hadn't had time to react. Now, I felt great waves of sadness coursing through my body. Shanti held out her hand.

'We can't stay here,' she told me. 'We'll get caught. We must keep moving, Arjan. Once my master realises what I've done, he will send men to kill us.'

I knew she was right, but the pain in my chest wouldn't stop. I wanted my dad. I was just a boy. How could I look after my family without him?

'Come on!' Shanti urged.

We left slowly, mostly because I held us up. Once outside, though, my determination returned.

'We should follow the tracks,' I told Shanti. 'It will take longer but they work around towards my district. It will be safer than taking the back streets and alleys again.'

Shanti nodded. 'That is where my master will send his thugs.'

I took her hand and smiled. 'Don't call him that any more. If something good has come from this terrible night, it's your freedom. He doesn't own you now.'

Her smile was wide and beaming.

'You are a good friend, Arjan, ' she replied. 'The only one I've ever had.'

I hugged her and then we continued on our way.

* * *

It was half a mile before I saw it. At first I thought it was a mirage – my mind playing tricks on me. But it was real enough. I pulled Shanti into some bushes and put a finger to her lips.

'Ssshhh!' I said, my heart jumping in my chest.

'What?' she whispered.

'Up ahead,' I told her excitedly. 'It's the night train!'

Chapter Thirteen

Finding Dad

Confused soldiers surrounded the train, trying to get used to the darkness. They seemed to be searching each compartment and some were even on the roof. Others crawled along the track, searching the underside of each carriage. I thought quickly.

'I have to get inside somehow,' I told Shanti.

'That's impossible,' she replied. 'They will see you.'

I shook my head. 'I can't let them. I thought I'd failed but now I've got another chance. I have to help my dad.'

The tracks lay between two steep banks that were overgrown with weeds. We used them as cover and moved along the left bank, edging closer to the train. I felt the firecrackers in my pockets and the matches I'd taken when I'd started my journey.

'If we let the firecrackers off, they'll think someone is attacking them,' I whispered to Shanti. 'Maybe they'll investigate and I can sneak down?'

Shanti didn't seem convinced.

'But it will be too dangerous,' she told me. 'They might shoot you.'

I told her my address and my mother's name. 'If anything happens to me, you go there and she'll help you.'

Shanti shook her head. 'No. We escaped together. Whatever happens now, we stay together.'

I nodded and pulled out the fireworks.

'We'll set them off along the ridge, back there.' I said. 'If we're quick, we can light them and run across the tracks to the far bank. When the soldiers investigate, we can get onto the train.'

We edged back about twenty yards and stood the crackers on the ground, each one about two feet apart. Then I set out a second row, parallel with the first. I could light two at a time that way. Starting with the ones farthest away, I got out my matches.

'Go now,' I told Shanti. 'Wait for me on the other bank.'

As she scampered across the tracks, I took a deep breath and lit my first match. The firecrackers had long wicks, so I managed to light several before the first two went bang. They were high-quality fireworks and the sound was almost deafening. White smoke billowed from them.

As the soldiers panicked and began to shout, I lit the rest and then hid in some bushes. All of them ran towards me, their rifles held out. I lit another cracker from my pockets and threw it further away from the tracks. When it exploded, the soldiers began to shoot into the gloom. I repeated my action three more times and then ran over to Shanti. In the darkness and confusion, we slipped past more armed men and made it to the train.

'That was great!' said Shanti.

'Wait here, then,' I said. 'I'll go and check each carriage.'

'No, I'll go first. If the soldiers see me, they won't shoot. I'm only a girl.'

She was right and I nodded. 'Alright. But the first sign of trouble and you run.'

The first carriage was empty, save for some suitcases and bags. In the second, we found food and medical supplies. I guessed that they were for the fort at Lahore, and had been sent from Delhi. The train was the main transport for soldiers across Northern India. That was why it was so heavily guarded. In the third carriage, there were wooden boxes, stamped with words in English, which I couldn't understand. There were so many that we had to squeeze past them.

At the end, there was no door – only a metal ladder that led us onto the roof. We took it and made our way to the fourth carriage. Behind us, I could hear the soldiers returning. Shanti heard them too.

'We must hurry!' she whispered.

We ran through three more carriages, all deserted, until we found the one we were looking for. It had no windows and the side doors were bolted shut. It had to be the prisoner transport coach.

The only way in was through doors at each end. And at the first stood a young guard, no more than eighteen years old. We crouched behind more boxes and Shanti told me it was her turn to help. I wanted to stop her but she insisted.

'I'll lead him this way. Once we pass you, check the carriage.'

'But what about you?'

She smiled. 'I'll meet you outside, at the top of the bank.'

Counting to three, she stood and ran to the guard, pretending to cry. 'Help!' she screamed. 'Please!'

The guard looked startled but when he saw Shanti he didn't raise his rifle.

'What are you doing here?' he asked.

'I've escaped from some bandits!' she wailed. 'They are after me. Come quickly – you must protect me!'

The soldier looked puzzled. 'What bandits?' he asked.

'They're outside,' she told him. 'Please! If they take me, I will be killed!'

The soldier's face changed. His eyes grew narrow and he raised his gun. 'Show me!' he demanded. 'Show me these dogs that would harm a child!'

Shanti turned and led him past me. As soon as they were gone, I stood and ran into the carriage. It was full of men, most sleeping on the rough floor. When they heard me enter, some of them woke up, blinking in the darkness.

'Dad?' I whispered. 'Dad – it's me, Arjan!'

For a moment no one replied but then I heard a voice that made my heart leap.

'Arjan – is that really you?' came my dad's voice. He sounded weak and tired.

'Come on!' I said. 'We have to go.'

And then he was at my side, his turban gone, and his long hair a mess. The right side of his face was swollen and the eye bruised over.

'What did they do?' I gasped.

I took his hand and we ran out, followed by some of the others.

'What are you doing here?' asked my dad.

'Never mind that now,' I told him. 'We have to leave before the soldiers come back.

At the door, two prisoners shoved past us and jumped down to the tracks. Before I could warn them, they ran towards the soldiers. I took my dad the other way, and we climbed the steep bank through thick weeds and bushes. I heard whistles blowing, soldiers shouting and the crack of three rifle shots. Someone screamed and then I heard more soldiers.

Shanti tapped me on the shoulder, making me start. My heart was almost in my mouth with excitement.

'What happened to the soldier?' I asked.

'He went to check some bushes and I hid,' she replied.

'You're very brave,' I told her. 'For a girl.'

Shanti shoved me as my father looked on in utter confusion.

'I don't understand what's happening,' he said. 'Is this a dream?'

Two more gunshots and the sound of a screaming, dying man told my dad it wasn't a dream – or a nightmare.

'Follow me,' said Shanti, standing up.

I helped my dad up, angered when I heard him groan in pain.

'Quickly!' Shanti whispered, leading us away from the tracks and back into the city before more patrols arrived.

Chapter Fourteen

Showdown

The rest of the journey was slow and I was beginning to get tired. My dad could only limp. We had to hide several times, to avoid being seen. Not only were we running from the soldiers and the police, we had The Bull's thugs to think about too. By now he would be searching every street for us, according to Shanti.

I wondered what we would do, even if we did make it home. My father was a wanted man, and if we stayed in Amritsar it was just a question of whether the police or The Bull would get us first.

Soon we were on familiar ground, as we skirted the marketplace. We didn't cut through, though, because I'd spotted some shady-looking men.

'Bandits!' I whispered to Shanti and my dad.

When she saw them, Shanti's face went pale. 'His men,' she said in disgust. 'I recognise them.'

I looked at my dad, who seemed to be close to passing out. A dark patch was growing on his side. When I touched it, I saw blood on my fingers.

'Dad?'

He shook his head. 'They wanted me to give them information,' he whispered, his voice hoarse. 'I tried to tell them I was innocent but...'

Shanti turned her head suddenly. 'No, God, *no*!'

'What's the matter?'

Shanti's eyes filled with tears. 'It's him! The Bull!'

He stood by the far end of the market square, carrying a kerosene lamp in his left hand. In his right was a length of thick rope. On the end of the rope was the nastiest-looking dog I had ever seen.

It had huge, powerful shoulders and a long snout, filled with sharp teeth. Its front paws were massive, almost too big for its body. It snapped and growled and The Bull's men seemed scared of it.

'He calls it Death,' she told me. 'I've seen it rip out a man's throat before.'

We were in serious trouble. Once the dog caught our scents, we were finished. We couldn't outrun it or its master. Not with my dad as injured as he was.

That was when I felt the air around us change. It grew thicker and warmer, and carried the scent of mangoes and fresh cream. Even before she appeared, I knew she would. Heera…

'I had a feeling we'd meet again,' she said. 'What is it about you and dogs, Arjan?'

'Heera!'

She smiled and looked at my father. 'You need attention, Mit Singh,' she told him. Then she saw Shanti. 'Hello, child. Aren't you a pretty thing?'

She saw a line of dirt on Shanti's left cheek, reached out and wiped it away. I thought Shanti would react but she seemed mesmerised. I looked back to the bandits. The Bull had them searching now, and he was giving the dog fabric to sniff.

'That's my top,' Shanti told me. 'The one I left behind.'

The dog's growl echoed in the empty square. It lurched from its master's hands and started to follow the scent trail. As it came closer, I could see how big it was.

'We must run!' I said to Heera.

She shook her head and told us to get behind her. Then she knelt down, just as the beast approached our hiding place. Behind it, the bandits continued to search too. The dog stopped ten yards short of us and bared its huge teeth but Heera was unfazed. Shanti began to sob, her hands shaking. I pulled her behind me.

'If it attacks, you run,' I whispered to her.

Heera took something from under her shawl. It was a simple tin whistle. She put it to her mouth and blew. I heard no noise but the dog seemed to. It cocked its massive head to one side and looked puzzled.

Suddenly, more dogs began to bark. A pack of them emerged from a lane across the square from us. I saw the leader – the same dogs that had cornered me earlier that night. The largest one snarled, and the others sprinted in our direction. The bandit's dog sensed them. It let out a low, deep rumbling growl and turned to face the stray pack. Within seconds it was surrounded – the strays biting and tearing at it. I heard The Bull call for a gun from his men.

'Come,' Heera told us. 'No one else will harm any of you tonight. You have my word.'

She put my dad's arm around her shoulder and we entered the dark alley where I'd first encountered her. I had so many questions but first we needed to be safe. The door to her dwelling was unlocked and we rushed inside.

'Lock it,' Heera told me.

The padlock was old and rusty and I wondered if it would keep the bandits out.

'Don't worry about them,' Heera said to me. 'No one enters this house without my permission. The Bull can wait for another day. He and I will have our reckoning when Fate decrees it.'

How did she do that – understand what I was thinking? And was there anyone in Amritsar she *didn't* know?

As she tended to my father's wounds, she told Shanti to light another candle and make some tea.

'We'll wait here until they leave,' she said. 'And I will answer those questions, Arjan. After tonight, this city will cease to be your home.'

* * *

Later, as both Shanti and my father slept, I sat with Heera and drank more tea. I was weary but I couldn't rest.

'What happened to the teenager you freed?' I asked her.

'Oh, he's safe. He is back with his family.'

'But why did you help him?'

Heera blew on her tea before replying. 'He is an innocent, just like your father.'

'And you saved him?'

Heera shook her head. 'I just did what people like me do,' she said, confusing me.

'What are you?' I asked. 'A witch?'

Again, she shook her head. 'No – I'm not a witch,' she said, smiling. 'Though many people call me such names.'

'So what then?'

She put down her cup and looked into my eyes. 'I watch over people in this city,' she explained. 'That is all.'

'Like a guardian angel?'

This time she laughed out loud. 'I have no wings. But something like that.'

'You never answer a question properly. Why?'

'Why not?' she told me. 'Besides, you need to listen.'

I raised an eyebrow. 'Listen to what?'

Heera picked up her cup and took a sip.

'Your family must leave Amritsar,' she said. 'You know this, don't you?'

I nodded. 'The bandits and the police will come for us.'

'The British too,' she added. 'It's unfair but that is the way of Life sometimes.'

'Where will we go?'

Heera found a pencil and a scrap of paper. 'Do you know exactly where your father's ancestral village is?'

I shook my head. She began to draw a map, marking out various places. When she was done, she gave it to me. 'You will follow this and leave the city, as soon as we get back to your mother.'

'But...'

She shook her head. 'In two days' time many people will die here. Hundreds of people. In the confusion, people will think you died too.'

'Why?' I asked, my eyes wide.

'It doesn't matter why,' she replied. 'It cannot be stopped.'

'How can you predict such things?'

Heera put a hand on my face. It felt smooth and cold.

'I can't say,' she said. 'All that matters is that you take your mother and your new friend to safety. That is your task, Arjan. Are you ready for it?'

I nodded.

'Good,' she said. 'This journey is almost over, my son. Now you start a new one. You must be brave and strong, Arjan. Your family will need it.'

We spoke some more and then my father opened his eyes. Heera explained what was happening and he nodded in sadness. I watched Shanti sleeping with her hair splayed out behind her, and wondered what Heera had meant. Why would I need to be strong for my family?

'Wake her,' Heera said to me. 'We must be at your house by sunrise.'

Chapter Fifteen

The Next Journey

So here I am. Packing with my mother. My father's injuries are worse than we thought. He is too ill to come with us. Heera is watching over him. When he's better, she will bring him to us.

Mr and Mrs Khan are sobbing now, and my mother is too. The sun is close to rising, and all around us people are preparing for work. It feels like any other day but it isn't.

Eventually, we set off. My mother sits next to me, wrapped in a blanket, as I guide the bullock and cart eastwards, away from the city and from the life we had. Shanti is hidden beneath more blankets in the back. The bandits will look for her. We cannot risk her being seen.

Heera has warned me that our journey will be dangerous. It will take many days and we will be travelling through open country. There will be more bandits and army patrols – more danger. She has told me to be brave – to be a man. I don't understand why, but I trust her. My heart is heavy and my stomach churns but I can't let my fears stop me. With my father so sick, I have to stand up. I must get my family to safety.

The night run is over. It is time for the next journey to begin.

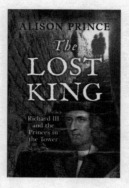

The Lost King

Alison Prince

The compelling story of Richard III and the disappearance
of the princes in the Tower.

A fascinating look at the brief reign of Richard III, told
by the princes' nursemaid. What really happened to the
princes in the Tower? Was Richard responsible – or has
he been wrongly accused for centuries?

ISBN 9781472904409   £5.99

The Girl From Hard Times Hill

Emma Barnes

A working-class girl in 1950s Britain struggles to cope with changes in her life when her father returns from Occupied Germany. When Megan wins a place at grammar school, she must learn to cope with a new town and a school where she doesn't fit in. Can Megan adapt to her new life, and take advantage of a changing Britain?

An emotional tale of growing up at a time of change.

ISBN 9781472904430   £5.99

Bring Out the Banners

Geoffrey Trease

Two young women from very different backgrounds
become unlikely friends as they struggle for women's
right to vote in the approach to the First World War.

A thrilling story of secret meetings, police oppression
and social upheaval, as well as an accurate account of the
Suffragette movement.

ISBN 9781408191866   £5.99